THIS SERIES OF BOOKS
IS DEDICATED TO THE MEMORY OF
ANNE-MARIE DALMAIS
WHOSE GREAT ENTHUSIASM
AND INSPIRATION MADE THIS
PROJECT COME TO LIFE

Four Little Friends

GYO FUJIKAWA

WELCOME, MEI SU
and other tales

Modern Publishing
A Division of Unisystems, Inc.
New York, New York 10022
Printed in Italy

WELCOME, MEI SU

Patsy hurried on her way
To meet her friends one sunny day.
As she did, she waved "hello"
To somebody she didn't know.

The boys were waiting at the spot
Where the three friends played a lot.
"Guess what!" excited Patsy cried
To Sam and Brian, grinning wide.

"There's a new girl in town,"
Said Patsy, jumping up and down.
"Let's go see if she will come
And play with us. We'll all have fun."

Brian pulled the welcome wagon.
Rags followed with his tail a-wagging!
The girl seemed sad and timid, too,
Till she smiled and said, "My name's Mei Su."

"Welcome to the neighborhood!
We came by and hoped you would
Come out to share our toys and play
With the three of us today."

They told her what they liked to do.
"We love to play dress-up—do you?
And sometimes we go berry picking,
Or play ball. Are you good at kicking?"

"Woof!" barked Rags. The new friends laughed.
They knew that their friendship would last.
Smiling happily, they agree,
Four little friends are better than three!

THAT'S NOT FAIR

Brian's little sister, Sarah,
Came with him to play one day.
"She's too small," said Patsy, frowning.
"She'll spoil things if we let her play."

Sam agreed, but Brian said,
"If Sarah goes, then I go, too.
Come on, Sarah, let's go home.
I'd rather play with you."

Mei Su knew how Brian felt.
She had a little brother.
"Let's be fair," she said. "We all
Can play with one another.

"There's lots of clothes Sarah can wear,
And games enough for five."
In the end the friends were glad
That Mei Su was so wise.

FLY BALL!

One day the four friends
   were out playing ball.
Brian swung the bat,
   and they all began to call,

"I've got it." "No, I have."
   "It's coming my way!"
They all ran together
   to make the play.

"Watch out!" Brian shouted.
"You're going to crash."
Too late—they all fell
into the wet grass.

Then the friends laughed
as Rags caught the ball.
"Look at that!" said Sam.
"Rags can outplay us all."

SNOWBALL DREAMS

We wished all day, and dreamed all night
That snow would come our way.
In the morning, the ground was white.
We rushed outside to play.

We built a great big snowman,
And played the whole day through.

We knew that friends who share a dream
Can make that dream come true!

SAM'S ALL-WRONG DAY

It started out an all-wrong day
As Sam jumped out of bed.
He stepped on Rags' tail,
And the poor dog yelped and fled.

He wondered how to make it right,
And to himself he said:

1 Take your time
2 Don't hurry
3 Don't be careless
4 Never worry
5 Be patient
6 Go slow
7 Be careful
8 Be thorough
9 Think things through, go step-by-step
10 Do things right, then take a rest!